Little Red Warrior and His Lawyer

Also by **Kevin Loring**
and published by Talonbooks

Thanks for Giving
Where the Blood Mixes

LITTLE RED WARRIOR AND HIS LAWYER

A TRICKSTER LAND CLAIM FABLE

a play by

KEVIN LORING

TALONBOOKS

Talonbooks
9259 Shaughnessy Street, Vancouver, British Columbia, Canada v6p 6r4
talonbooks.com

Talonbooks is located on xʷməθkʷəy̓əm, Skwx̱wú7mesh, and səl̓ilwətaʔɬ Lands.

First printing: 2021

Typeset in Arno
Printed and bound in Canada on 100% post-consumer recycled paper

Interior and cover design by Typesmith
Cover image: *A Subjugation of Truth* by Kent Monkman

Talonbooks acknowledges the financial support of the Canada Council for the Arts, the Government of Canada through the Canada Book Fund, and the Province of British Columbia through the British Columbia Arts Council and the Book Publishing Tax Credit.

Rights to produce *Little Red Warrior and His Lawyer*, in whole or in part, in any medium by any group, amateur or professional, are retained by the author. Interested persons are requested to contact the author care of Talonbooks at info@talonbooks.com.

LIBRARY AND ARCHIVES CANADA CATALOGUING IN PUBLICATION

Title: Little Red Warrior and his lawyer : a trickster land claim fable / Kevin Loring.
Names: Loring, Kevin, 1974– author.
Identifiers: Canadiana 2021011939X | ISBN 9781772012545 (softcover)
Subjects: LCGFT: Drama.
Classification: LCC PS8623.O743 L58 2021 | DDC C812/.6—dc23

This play is dedicated to the Warriors fighting for Indigenous Rights, for the well-being of their communities and for Mother Earth. kʷukʷstéyp.

PLAYWRIGHT'S PREFACE

I wanted to tell a Story about Land Claims from the perspective of snk̓ýép, Coyote, our sacred profane Trickster, as told in the Nlaka'pamux Story Traditions. Not to adhere to any kind of ethnographic accuracy, but to write a play imbued with the spirit of those Coyote Stories.

Coyote Stories are a part of our sptékʷɬ Stories, about animal beings with human aspects who are presented in our Creation or Foundational Stories. These characters represent all of the animals within Nlaka'pamux cultural knowledge and the specific fauna found on our Lands, Coyote being the most powerful and consequential of them. Other animals like Rabbit are also Tricksters, but they have traits that differentiate them from snk̓ýép. The Coyote character in Nlaka'pamux culture is vain, selfish in the extreme, cunning, lustful, arrogant, foolish, greedy, and vengeful. He embodies the worst of human character. And that makes him funny. But he is also a powerful transformer, a shape-shifter, a conjurer, and a lover.

In the Coyote Stories there is Old Man Coyote, who is malevolent and often trying to sleep with the three gorgeous duck wives of his son, the younger Coyote. Old Man Coyote tricks his son into going on a trans-dimensional journey into the Sky Nation that takes eight years to return from. All so that he can sleep with his son's wives. And through his triumphs and follies on the journey back home, Coyote transforms the world into the reality we recognize today. In other adventures, Coyote has conversations with combs and blankets, deep philosophical conversations with his own asshole, and transforms his feces into various desirable objects in order to trick a cannibal or some other unsuspecting powerful being out of their possessions.

This play is inspired by these ancient, hilarious, absurd Stories that on closer investigation reveal a rich narrative imbued with absolutely deliberate cultural memes, reflecting the Beliefs and Laws of the people. The Trickster behaves in ways counter to the Customs and Beliefs of the people, thereby provoking them not to live by his example but to enjoy and understand his faults in relation to their Values and Laws. His misdeeds shape the world around us.

I wanted to explore that kind of contrary Trickster dramaturgy in the context of a Land Claim. What would Coyote do if his Lands were being threatened? Yet no character in this play is named Coyote or snk̓y̓ép; rather, the Trickster is the universe of this play. Transformation is possible, nothing is certain, and everyone is suspect. In Trickster Stories, no one walks away unscathed.

LITTLE RED WARRIOR
AND HIS LAWYER

PRODUCTION HISTORY

Little Red Warrior and His Lawyer was first produced on March 24, 2001, with the following cast and crew:

LITTLE RED WARRIOR	Stuart Pierre
LARRY	Corey Turner
DESDEMONA	Sonja Bennett
FLOYD	David Richmond-Peck

Director	Michael McLaughlin
Stage Manager	Lisa Phillippe
Set Designer	Craig Hall
Costume Designer	Tyler Tone
Lighting Designer	Shaun August
Dramaturge	Alex Poch-Goldin
	Aaron Bushkowsky
Production Manager	Carol Chrisjohn
Technical Director	Bruce Kennedy

Little Red Warrior and His Lawyer was first commissioned by Studio 58 (Artistic Director, Kathryn Shaw). Later drafts were commissioned by Western Canada Theatre and Savage Society.

CHARACTERS

LITTLE RED WARRIOR, the Chief and last remaining member of his Tribe, the Little Red Warrior First Nation.

LARRY the lawyer, Little Red Warrior's court-appointed lawyer with big dreams of one day impressing his wife, Desdemona.

DESDEMONA, a ruthless, high-powered real-estate broker and lawyer. She is far more successful than her limp husband, Larry. When Little Red Warrior gifts her the "Indian name" FLANNEL DANCER, she begins to transform into a mighty pretendian.

FLOYD, a transformer and the storyteller of this tale. A patriarchal and commanding figure, he transforms into the engineer developing Little Red Warrior's Land. He also transforms into JUDGE BIG WILLY, who punishes Little Red Warrior for trying to protect his Land. He is the voice of the Ancestors when Larry has a vision. He becomes LOWER COURT FLOYD for the first Land Claim trial, APPEALS COURT FLOYD when Larry and Little Red Warrior appeal, and SUPREME COURT FLOYD for the final judgment. As Floyd is both the antagonist and the knowledge keeper of this story, everything is suspect.

THE QUEEN, the seductive and slightly cannibalistic drag manifestation of colonial power and the grand deity of the colonies.

SCENE 1

Prologue

FLOYD enters; he appears as a homeless person pushing a shopping cart full of pop cans and bottles. LARRY walks past him drinking a coffee, looking at his watch – he's late.

FLOYD
For five bucks, I'll tell you a story. It's a good story.

LARRY crosses past FLOYD.

LARRY
Out of my way! I'm late.

FLOYD
(*to the audience*) How about you folks? You wanna hear a story? Obviously. I mean, you're here, right? Well, hold on to your pantaloons, it's a gooder. This is the story of Little Red Warrior and His Lawyer.

Banjo music with a beat plays. Lights up, revealing LITTLE RED WARRIOR sitting in his chair.

FLOYD
Little Red Warrior lived a humble, reclusive life on his Ancestral Lands, in his little Red Shack, foraging and

hunting in the woods and fishing in the Little Red Lake.
He rarely ventured into town except to pick up his cheque.

*LITTLE RED WARRIOR pantomimes
throughout. He now gets up and mimes
exiting a door.*

FLOYD
It was the first week of spring, the sun was shining, the
birds were chirping, and the bunny rabbits were mating.
All this brought a great big smile to Little Red's big ruby
cheeks. As Little Red walked towards the other side of
the lake, he began to hear strange sounds. The sounds of
industry. As he got closer, he was surprised to see that
there were several white trailers set up like a tiny village
along the edge of the lake. A road had been cut through
his forest like a scar, and on it drove big white trucks, and
in those trucks were big white men, and all around there
were great big machines chewing up his peaceful valley.

LITTLE RED WARRIOR
Holy shit!

FLOYD
It had only been a few weeks since his last visit to the
village, how could this invasion be happening, he thought.
From deep down in his spirit, a passion welled up inside
him. The outrage of his Ancestors possessed his body.
On he charged, into the tiny white village, until he came
upon a man with a white hard hat.

*FLOYD digs into his shopping cart and
retrieves a white hard hat. LITTLE RED
WARRIOR confronts FLOYD.*

LITTLE RED WARRIOR
(*to FLOYD*) What the hell are you doing here?!

FLOYD
We're developing this entire valley. Condos, beautiful townhouses and condos. Lakefront property. Pristine wilderness backwater … great selling features. Now, if you'll excuse me, you're trespassing.

LITTLE RED WARRIOR
(*turning back to the audience*) Trespassing?

FLOYD
There would be no containing the rage of the Little Red Warrior.

LITTLE RED WARRIOR
Trespassing?!

FLOYD
The burning blister that had been building up in his belly exploded. The fury of all the Red Warriors that had come before him rushed through Red's body. Generations of anguish channelled into one singular moment of retaliation.

LITTLE RED WARRIOR
Little Red smash!!

> *LITTLE RED WARRIOR hits FLOYD over the head with a shovel. A loud gong. Thunder and lightning. Sirens. The world is suddenly awash in red. The set transforms around LITTLE RED WARRIOR, as the sounds and*

*imagery of protests past, present, and future
are projected all across the set and news reports
of Indigenous unrest cut in and out. LITTLE
RED WARRIOR stands still as his world is
torn from him, to be replaced by a room at the
local police station. LITTLE RED WARRIOR
is now waiting to be interviewed by his court-
appointed lawyer.*

SCENE 2

Penal Love

LARRY enters.

LARRY
Hi, I'm Larry. I'll be your lawyer. You must be, (*shuffling through papers*) uh ... Red? Little Red? Ah, here we are: assault, battery, destruction of property ...

LITTLE RED WARRIOR
I don't got no money, so you might as well crawl on back to the hole you came from.

LARRY
I'm your court-appointed lawyer. So the government is paying for my fees –

LITTLE RED WARRIOR
Who's paying the government?

LARRY
Taxpayers, I guess.

LITTLE RED WARRIOR
I don't pay taxes.

LARRY
Of course you don't ... of course ... So, you're charged
with assault and battery, trespassing –

LITTLE RED WARRIOR
Trespassing?! They're on my Land!

LARRY
Well, it appears that the development firm Smith, Smyth,
and Goldesmithe has legal title to the Land in question –

LITTLE RED WARRIOR
Legal title? Says who?! Who the hell do they
think they are?

LARRY
They are the plaintiffs. They claim that they were attacked
by you, whom they describe as "a radical Indigenous anti-
establishment gorilla."

LITTLE RED WARRIOR
That's racist! Can I sue them for that?

LARRY
No.

LITTLE RED WARRIOR
Some lawyer you are ...

LARRY
Now look, you're charged with assault with a shovel. You
put a man in the hospital, now I need to know: Why?
Were you (*pause*) intoxicated?

LITTLE RED WARRIOR
No.

LARRY
Sure?

LITTLE RED WARRIOR
Yes!

LARRY
Okay, all right, just checking. Now, for our "relationship"
to work you must listen to me. Okay? I tell you what you
need to do and say to get you off the hook. And you do
and say what I tell you to. That is the only way this is going
to work. Do you understand?

LITTLE RED WARRIOR
I understand.

LARRY
Good.

LITTLE RED WARRIOR
I understand that you're a colonizer.

LARRY
Oh, for Christ's sake.

LITTLE RED WARRIOR
No, for my sake!

LARRY
I'm here to help you.

LITTLE RED WARRIOR

Yeah well, you said, "for Christ's sake." You guys already tried him, remember? And look where that got us.

LARRY

Now, now, I personally had nothing to do with that awful bit of history ... so please, let's stick to the issue at hand. Oh, unless of course you want to disclose any abuse, that may be helpful to your case. Were you ... you know, touched ... by a servant of god?

LITTLE RED WARRIOR

Back off!

LARRY

You can tell me, it'll be completely confidential, then you can spill the beans on the stand. Get it all out in the open. Record it on the record, your deepest, darkest, most painful moments, for posterity and the education of the proletariat.

LITTLE RED WARRIOR

Get licked! All you lawyer types are so ever sick! Just look at you.

LARRY

Excuse me?

LITTLE RED WARRIOR

I bet it takes you hours to put yourself together, don't it? You wake up, do your hair, put on your fancy little suit, just so you can look me in the eye and not have to flinch. I bet you drive one of them fancy European cars, don't you? Makes you feel like a real winner, innit? (*closing his eyes and putting his hand up in front of LARRY's face and*

psychically searching for the answer) BMW? Mercedes?
Vulva? You drive one of them fancy vulva cars! Black! It's
black, innit? You drive a black vulva!

LARRY
It's a ... Volvo, and no ... it's grey.

LITTLE RED WARRIOR
Hah! A grey vulva! I can see right through you!

LARRY
Look, you don't have to like me. But you still have to get
through this trial. And your best bet is to listen to me.

LITTLE RED WARRIOR
I am the last remaining member of my Tribe. Therefore,
I am Chief. And since I am a Chief and you are merely
a lawyer, I don't have to listen to you or anybody else.
I wanna talk to the Queen!

LARRY
Delusional! Perfect! We'll enter an insanity plea. The judge
will send you to a mental institution for evaluation. And
now that all the loony bins have been shut down, you'll be
back on the streets in no time!

LITTLE RED WARRIOR
I wanna to talk to the Queen!

LARRY
You can't talk to the Queen.

LITTLE RED WARRIOR
Why not, she too good for me?

LARRY

The Queen doesn't talk to just anybody. Besides, even if you could see her, it wouldn't do any good.

LITTLE RED WARRIOR

What do you mean?

LARRY

The Queen doesn't have any real power.

LITTLE RED WARRIOR

What are you talking about? She got her picture on the money!

LARRY

She's a symbol, a figurehead, a remnant of our once-glorious and homogenous empire.

LITTLE RED WARRIOR

How stupid do you think I am? Hello, "British Columbia"!

LARRY

You can't talk to the Queen!

LITTLE RED WARRIOR

But –

LARRY

– Trust me on this one, okay chief? Now, I realize this might be a hard one for you to comprehend, but this is the twenty-first century. Now, I think I've got an idea on how to approach this case. I can keep you from going to jail, but you need to take my advice. Now tell me about your mother.

LITTLE RED WARRIOR
What?

LARRY
Your father, then. Is there a history of abuse in your
family? Intergenerational? Perhaps you were a beaten and
battered child, you've got that ward-of-the-state aura about
you, give me the dirt, come on, something gut-wrenching.
We need sympathy if we're going to win this. So lay it on
me. Come on, I can take it. You can cry with me. I won't
judge you.

LITTLE RED WARRIOR
I feel sorry for you.

LARRY
You feel sorry for me? You live in a shack in the bush. You
don't even have running water. Oh, good one! (*taking out
a pen and pad and beginning to write notes*) No running
water, ward of the state, neglected by parents –

LITTLE RED WARRIOR
I wasn't never no ward of no state! I don't need you, and I
don't need your shyster lawyering! I can figure this thing
out on my own. I've seen this type of thing a million
times ... I've got cable.

LARRY
Oh, all right. Okay. No problemo, buddy boy. (*packing
up his briefcase and heading for the door*) You know, that
man you put in the hospital works for one of the largest
development firms in the country. That means money, lots
of it. Something you know nothing about. That lake you
lived on will be developed, and that outhouse you called a
home will be demolished. Without me, you will go to jail.

Your whole way of life has been taken from you. And now,
you are going to a nice, cold, concrete jail cell. If you think
you can take it. Have yourself a good day, sir.

>   *LARRY goes to leave.*

LITTLE RED WARRIOR
Ewww, the big bad lawyer gonna go home to his designer
home. Ewww, he's soo bad. La la la la laa ...

LARRY
Now, you listen to me, buddy, because you really need
to understand the situation here as it pertains to your
incarceration. I am the only thing between you and the
throbbing phallus of the Canadian penal system.

LITTLE RED WARRIOR
Throbbing phallus?

LARRY
Prison love, my brother, prison love ...

LITTLE RED WARRIOR
Oh.

>   *A pause as LITTLE RED WARRIOR
>   considers this.*

LARRY
Oh?

LITTLE RED WARRIOR
OH!

LARRY
Oh yeah, buddy boy! I hope you're not too shy, because if you keep this up, you're headed straight for the iron snuggle box.

LITTLE RED WARRIOR
Hey, give a guy a break, man. My whole world has just been turned upside down. And you come in here all pale and shysty! Look, I'm ...

LARRY
Say it.

LITTLE RED WARRIOR
I'm.

LARRY
Mmm hmm?

LITTLE RED WARRIOR
I'm ... shmorrrrrry ...

LARRY
What?

LITTLE RED WARRIOR
I'm shhmorrrrrrrry ...

LARRY
Pardon me?!

LITTLE RED WARRIOR
I'm sorry! Okay! I'm sorry! I need your help.

LARRY
Oh, now you're sorry. Well, "sorry" isn't gonna cut it, chief.

LARRY goes to leave.

LITTLE RED WARRIOR
No, come on, man, I's just testing you, see how tough and shysty you are. Can't just have anybody represent me, I'm the last of my people, I *am* royalty. Now come on. Times a-wasting, the iron snuggle box is getting closer.

LARRY
What's the matter, can't handle the penal love?

LITTLE RED WARRIOR
No, that sounds good. It's the snuggle box that's got me creeped out. Truce?

LARRY
Okay then, truce, no bullshit.

LITTLE RED WARRIOR
Okay.

LARRY
Now tell me, why did you assault this man?

LITTLE RED WARRIOR
Those bastards are digging up my Land! How would you like it if I crawled into your backyard and started ripping everything up with bulldozers and chainsaws –

LARRY
Okay, okay, so you were protecting your property –

LITTLE RED WARRIOR
I was kicking his ass. He had no right to be there.
Nobody asked me.

LARRY
Do you have documents proving the Land belongs to you?

LITTLE RED WARRIOR
My Ancestors have been there since Time Immemorial.

LARRY
(*thinking*) Right, right ... but do you have proof?

LITTLE RED WARRIOR
Their bones in the ground are proof enough. For
thousands of years, we Little Red Warriors have been
there. Harvesting the bitter roots of the mountain, fishing
trout from the lake, getting our blood sucked by the
leaches and mosquitoes, our skin shredded and our eyes
torn from their sockets by the branches and little thorny
needles that go in but never come out. We're a part of that
valley. I am that valley!

LARRY
This development deal they're planning is worth a
lot of money.

LITTLE RED WARRIOR
I don't care about the stupid white man's – how
much money?

LARRY
Millions, maybe tens of millions, no, hundreds of millions!

LITTLE RED WARRIOR
So many millions …

LARRY
As I understand it, they're building a ski resort with a quaint little boutique village by the lake.

LITTLE RED WARRIOR
But nobody asked me! They can't do that and not ask me! That's Red Warrior Land!

LARRY
I think we have grounds for a Land Claim. We can get your Land back and justify your attack on that engineer if we can prove that you have title to the Land. You were just protecting your property! I wonder why they didn't check the records for Traditional Use Claims by your people.

LITTLE RED WARRIOR
Well, it's just me. I am my people. Probably nobody cared, only one Indian.

LARRY
Will you take my advice?

LITTLE RED WARRIOR
I'm up shit creek already, might as well bring a lawyer along.

LARRY
Excellent!

LARRY begins to write up a contract.

LITTLE RED WARRIOR
How come you're so eager now, anyways? What's in
it for you?

LARRY
Well, I'll get my usual legal fees and, oh – sign here.

> *LARRY hands LITTLE RED WARRIOR the*
> *contract. LITTLE RED WARRIOR signs.*

LARRY
Sixty-five percent of all capital and assets pertaining to this
Land deal.

LITTLE RED WARRIOR
Crook!

> *LITTLE RED WARRIOR lunges for*
> *LARRY's neck. They freeze in mid-*
> *strangulation/argument. FLOYD enters.*

FLOYD
And so Larry the lawyer and Little Red Warrior became ...
partners. It wasn't easy; they fought each other tooth
and nail for a day and a night, until finally they came to a
mutual understanding.

> *LITTLE RED WARRIOR and*
> *LARRY unfreeze.*

LARRY
I love you, man.

LITTLE RED WARRIOR
No man, I love you!

LITTLE RED WARRIOR and LARRY hug.

FLOYD
Having settled their personal differences, Larry posted bail for his new client.

> *LARRY writes out a cheque and gives it to FLOYD, who has now donned a judge's wig.*

FLOYD
Thank you. Okay, buh-bye.

> *FLOYD waves LITTLE RED WARRIOR and LARRY away. They cross downstage talking silently to each other.*

FLOYD
Now, bonded, there remained yet one obstacle to their newborn partnership.

LITTLE RED WARRIOR
I got no place to stay –

FLOYD
But the ever-resourceful Larry had it all figured out.

LARRY
Don't worry, Red, I've got it all figured out.

> *LITTLE RED WARRIOR and LARRY exit.*

SCENE 3

Capitulation

FLOYD
Enter Desdemona.

DESDEMONA enters, as if driving a car, and talking business on her cellphone.

FLOYD
A young urban professional, just like her husband – a lawyer, in fact. Beautiful, intelligent, terrifying, a well-put-together façade hiding a soft, vulnerable inner core –

DESDEMONA nearly runs FLOYD over.

DESDEMONA
Get off the goddamn road, moron!

LARRY enters and DESDEMONA pulls up beside him. FLOYD exits.

DESDEMONA
Hi honey.

LARRY gets into the car.

LARRY

Hi. Sorry you had to pick me up, but the vulva – ah, the car got towed.

DESDEMONA

There oughta be a law! Kiss, kiss. How was your day?

LARRY

Well, a murderer who did it for god, a dealer who did it for love, and a Native guy who did it because they stole his Land.

DESDEMONA

Well, we're in the right business. There'll never be a shortage of losers.

LARRY

I know we've talked about bringing work home and the strain that brings to our relationship, but ... I invited the Native guy to stay with us.

DESDEMONA

Pardon?

LARRY

It'll only be for a little while.

DESDEMONA

Are you crazy?! No way! How could you?! We don't know anything about him. We don't know where he's been! He could be a criminal!

LARRY
He is, dear, that's why he's here. But he's a righteous
criminal. He's the Chief of a small First Nation. In fact, he's
the only remaining member. He's basically an endangered
species. Anyways, I'm having him released into my
custody. Watch that woman with the five kids walking
across the –

DESDEMONA nearly runs over the family.
She yells at them out the window.

DESDEMONA
What freaking country are you in?! Walks right out into
traffic waving her hands like that'll stop me! I tell you,
it's like a Hobbesian nightmare. *Leviathan*! *Leviathan*!
Seriously! I'm not racist, but having escaped from
whatever Third World dictatorship they come from, they
should at least be more eager to acquire the subtle nuances
of the country that has embraced them. It's fucking with
my chakras.

LARRY
Anyways, I have an obligation to make sure that he's taken
care of while he's in the city.

DESDEMONA
Since when does being a lawyer require you to care for
your clients? Isn't there some government program or
something that can help him out? This is still a welfare
state, isn't it?

LARRY
Honey ... I'm a crown-appointed lawyer. Benevolence.

DESDEMONA breathes deeply.

DESDEMONA
Benevolence.

LARRY
The least you could do is support me. I'm being WOKE here! Besides, I'm also protecting my investment.

DESDEMONA
You're investing in rare Aboriginals?

LARRY
Listen, we've got a Land deal in the making. I don't want some other shyster lawyer stealing this opportunity from me. I need to keep an eye on him. If I win this case, we'll get 65 percent of the assets pertaining to this Land deal. Kind of a "you scratch me, I'll scratch you" type of thingy.

DESDEMONA
Is that the legal definition or a rash you're dealing with?

LARRY
You just need to have a little faith. If this deal works out the way I plan, we'll be set. We could have anything we want! New cars, a boat, that chalet in the mountains with the big moose head over the fireplace, like we talked about. Hell, we could even afford children!

DESDEMONA
Children? In this market?

LARRY
It's been … three years now, and you know, you're …
mother isn't getting any younger, who knows how
long she'll be around, it'd be nice for her to have some
grandchildren to enjoy in her golden years. Besides, it'll
do us good.

*DESDEMONA hangs her head out the
window and yells at another driver.*

DESDEMONA
BASTARD!

DESDEMONA
It'll do *us* good? Do you have any idea what pregnancy
will do to this body? Let alone my career. It'll do *us*
good, my ass.

LARRY
Honey, pregnancy is a beautiful process.

DESDEMONA
Gestating a parasite the size of a watermelon in my uterus
is not my idea of a beautiful process, thank you very much.

LARRY
You would think of our child as a parasite?

DESDEMONA
How can any self-respecting career woman instill fear in
the hearts of her competition with an eight-pound pre-
lingual hominid hanging off her left breast! It's unnatural.
What if it turned out like your relatives, oh god? It would
be like a never-ending chain of scum-sucking vermin,
feeding off itself and those closest to it.

DESDEMONA and LARRY come to a stoplight.

LARRY
Honey! Ouch!

DESDEMONA
Well ...

LARRY
It would be a family.

DESDEMONA
It would be an abomination!

LARRY
This is a family we're talking about, not a mutating colony of parasites.

DESDEMONA
What's the difference? Besides, how am I going to get pregnant, I mean, ever since I got promoted at the firm you can't even –

LARRY
You didn't have to go there ...

The stoplight goes green.

DESDEMONA
Oh Larry, I'm sorry. It's just that ...

LARRY

You're overreacting. Listen, the only thing you need to
worry about is what we're going to do with all the money
I'm going to make off of this Land deal, okay? We're
talking multimillions. Multi. *Mul-ti*. So just you relax and
think of all the wonderful things we'll be able to buy.

DESDEMONA

Larry, with my job at the firm we don't need to
worry about –

LARRY

Diamonds and furs, Rolex and Gucci, Mercedes and –

DESDEMONA

Larry –

LARRY

Things. Lots of things. Big things. Expensive things.
Wonderful shiny things. Just you wait. We'll have
everything we always wanted. We'll be happy. It'll be
great. What do you say?

DESDEMONA

Oh, he can stay in the basement, if it'll make you happy,
as long as I don't have to deal with him.

LARRY

Thanks, honey. Everything will work out just fine,
you'll see.

DESDEMONA and LARRY go to kiss.

LARRY
Red. Red! RED LIGHT!

*The sound of tires screeching and a loud crash
as the car rear-ends another vehicle.*

DESDEMONA
Stupid bus driver! Where'd he learn to drive? Oh, I broke
a nail. Look ...

LARRY puts his hand to his neck.

LARRY
Ow!

SCENE 4

Hostess with the Mostess

Larry and Desdemona's house. Morning.
A table with chairs. DESDEMONA enters,
tidying up. LITTLE RED WARRIOR enters.
He watches her for a while.

LITTLE RED WARRIOR
Hey there.

DESDEMONA
(*startled*) Holy shit!

LITTLE RED WARRIOR
Uh, Larry gave me a key, so I just –

DESDEMONA
(*trying to regain composure*) I nearly tossed my pancakes.
Well, so, you must be –

LITTLE RED WARRIOR
Red, Little Red. Nice place you've got here.

DESDEMONA
Thank you, it must be … quite a shock, to be in a house
that is so much more …

LITTLE RED WARRIOR
IKEA? Wow, fancy.

DESDEMONA
Uh, no, not. Ah, so, well, I guess –

LITTLE RED WARRIOR
I brought you guys a gift. You know, for having me
stay here.

> *LITTLE RED WARRIOR hands*
> *DESDEMONA a soggy paper bag.*

DESDEMONA
Oh. How nice. (*examining the sticky package*) Um,
what is it?

LITTLE RED WARRIOR
q̓ʷúneʔ, fermented salmon eggs.

DESDEMONA
Oh dear.

LITTLE RED WARRIOR
It's a delicacy.

DESDEMONA
Oh no.

LITTLE RED WARRIOR
Yeah. Tastes kinda like cheese, only more rotten
and fishier.

DESDEMONA
Oh. Wow. Okay.

LITTLE RED WARRIOR
Yeah. With a subtle creamy texture on the tongue, too.

DESDEMONA
Why?

LITTLE RED WARRIOR
Huh?

DESDEMONA
Why. Thank ... you. I think.

LITTLE RED WARRIOR
Yeah. Old family recipe, hey. We wrap the egg sacs in
skunk cabbage leaves and then bury it in a sandy hole
for about two weeks, and then we dig it up and ... mmm
mmm mmm. But you gotta be careful, eh. A little too long
in the ground and, well ... salmon-ella.

> *LITTLE RED WARRIOR laughs.*
> *DESDEMONA doesn't.*

LITTLE RED WARRIOR
Get it?

DESDEMONA
No. Yeah. Ha. Good one.

Silence. DESDEMONA and LITTLE RED WARRIOR stare at each other. DESDEMONA delivers the toxic bag of rotten fish guts to a safe location for later disposal.

LITTLE RED WARRIOR
So you're his wife, eh?

DESDEMONA
Yeah, yes, yup, mm-hmm, oh, how rude of me. I'm Desdemona. But my friends call me Des. Or Mona.

LITTLE RED WARRIOR
Mona eh? That's funny, "moan, aaaah."

DESDEMONA
Right, so I understand that you live alone in the forest. That must be very ... lonely.

LITTLE RED WARRIOR
Nah, I like it. Peaceful, you know. The mountain air is so clean and fresh you can smell a moose fart for miles. Besides, I got cable.

DESDEMONA
I see.

Beat.

So, my husband tells me that you're an endangered species. I mean, that you're the only one left from your, uh, genus ...

LITTLE RED WARRIOR
Well, I'm no Einstein, but I got my GED.

DESDEMONA
NICE! Well, how about I show you your room?

LITTLE RED WARRIOR
Okay! Oh wait, hold on. Oh jeez.

DESDEMONA
What?

LITTLE RED WARRIOR
Come here for a second.

>*DESDEMONA crosses cautiously.*

DESDEMONA
What is it?

>*LITTLE RED WARRIOR puts his hand on DESDEMONA's head.*

LITTLE RED WARRIOR
Hold still.

DESDEMONA
Is something wrong? A bug, oh my god, do I have something in my teeth?

>*LITTLE RED WARRIOR examines DESDEMONA.*

LITTLE RED WARRIOR
Shh, I'm looking at you.

DESDEMONA
Oh.

LITTLE RED WARRIOR
Mmm hmm.

DESDEMONA
What?

LITTLE RED WARRIOR
Look this way.

DESDEMONA
Uh –

LITTLE RED WARRIOR
Now look that way ... yup, that's what I thought.

DESDEMONA
What is it?

LITTLE RED WARRIOR
(*pointing at her eyes*) You got a lazy eye.

DESDEMONA
Excuse me?

LITTLE RED WARRIOR
Oh yeah. It's only slightly lazy, but this one is definitely
not as active as that one.

DESDEMONA
Nobody's ever said that to me before.

LITTLE RED WARRIOR
They probably never wanted to upset you.

DESDEMONA
A lazy eye, I've never had a lazy anything! How can
this be? I look at myself in the mirror every day. I look
perfectly normal. PERFECTLY!

LITTLE RED WARRIOR
Maybe you're only seeing what you want to, you know,
projecting?

DESDEMONA
Oh, bullshit!

LITTLE RED WARRIOR
Bullshit or not, you're cockeyed.

DESDEMONA
Maybe it's only recently they've been like this, you know?
I've been under a lot of stress. In all my old photos I
look fine.

> DESDEMONA finds a compact and looks
> into the mirror.

DESDEMONA
I have been getting these dizzy spells, though. Maybe
they're related.

LITTLE RED WARRIOR
Could be from a lot of things, could be your life is
unfulfilled somehow, and your spirit is searching for a new
path other than the one that's right in front of you ...

DESDEMONA
What?

LITTLE RED WARRIOR
Could mean you gotta get an eyepatch. Helps balance 'em
out. Don't worry, I used to have one as a kid. You don't
look too weird. But it's awkward trying to figure out which
eye I'm supposed to look into. Eyepatch really simplifies
things. Where did you say my room was?

DESDEMONA points offstage.

LITTLE RED WARRIOR
Right.

*LITTLE RED WARRIOR scrutinizes
DESDEMONA from afar.*

DESDEMONA
WHAT?!

LITTLE RED WARRIOR
Nothing.

LITTLE RED WARRIOR exits.

DESDEMONA
I'm defective?!

DESDEMONA exits.

SCENE 5

Big Willy

FLOYD enters wearing a judge's robe.

FLOYD
And thus it came to pass that Little Red, Desdemona, and Larry came together. Little Red moved into the basement as Larry prepared to liberate Red from his assault charge.

LARRY and LITTLE RED WARRIOR enter.
LARRY is wearing a neck brace.

FLOYD
The Right Honourable Judge Big Willy presiding.

FLOYD puts on a judge's wig and becomes
JUDGE BIG WILLY.

JUDGE BIG WILLY
I'll now see the case! Little Red Warrior versus the developers Smith, Smythe, and Goldsmithe! What is your plea?

LARRY
Not guilty, Your Honourableship.

JUDGE BIG WILLY
Oh, really?

LARRY
He was defending his Land, Your Honour.

JUDGE BIG WILLY
Land Defender, eh?! You got any proof that said Land
belongs to you and your ancient, long-dead Ancestors?!

> LITTLE RED WARRIOR *pulls out a very*
> *large bone.*

LITTLE RED WARRIOR
This femur belongs to my great-great-great-grandfather's
great-uncle's aunt.

JUDGE BIG WILLY
Wow. She was a big one, eh?

LITTLE RED WARRIOR
They say we used to be giants back in the old days.
Over the years we shrunk. I guess colonization made us
smaller, eh.

LARRY
Uh, it was found on an ancient burial site of his people,
Your Honour, upon the Land that Smith, Smythe, and
Goldsmithe plan to develop into a golf course. We were
able to extract the mitochondrial DNA from this sample
and match it to Little Red's. The analysis concludes that
Red here is a direct descendant of this Ancestor.

LITTLE RED WARRIOR
We're claiming that Land. It's mine.

JUDGE BIG WILLY
LAND CLAIM?! Ha! Good luck! We'll all be dead by the
time that gets sorted out!

LARRY
Uh, Your Honourableness, I realize that in a realistic time
frame this dilemma would never be resolved, but you see,
sir, we are not dealing with a realistic time frame ...

LITTLE RED WARRIOR
People are watching.

JUDGE BIG WILLY notices the audience.

JUDGE BIG WILLY
Oh, yes, there is that, isn't there? Hi. How you doing?
We're really glad you all could join us tonight. We're
especially excited for the support of our subscribers. And
of course for the funders who paid for this production.
Thank you. (*turning back to the play*) Well, you had better
hope that this mess is all sorted out good and quick,
or these nice folks here won't give a rat's ass about you or
your stupid unoriginal rights. Now come here, boy. Are
you sorry for putting that nice man in the hospital over
your ridiculous, self-righteous political agenda?

LITTLE RED WARRIOR
Sorry?

LARRY
He is, Your Honour. He's very, very sorry. Aren't you, Red?

LITTLE RED WARRIOR
I –

LARRY

– am sorry. You see, Your Honour? Complete compliance.

JUDGE BIG WILLY

Well, good. Okay then. Hands.

LITTLE RED WARRIOR

What?

JUDGE BIG WILLY

Come on now, be a good lad and let me see your hands.

> *LITTLE RED WARRIOR holds his hands*
> *out, palms up. Schubert's "Ave Maria" begins*
> *to play. JUDGE BIG WILLY pulls out a belt*
> *and straps LITTLE RED WARRIOR's hands*
> *in slow motion.*

LITTLE RED WARRIOR

Ow! Little Red smash!!

LARRY

No!!

> *LITTLE RED WARRIOR retaliates.*
> *He grabs the bone of his Ancestor he brought*
> *into the courtroom and uses it to try to*
> *bludgeon JUDGE BIG WILLY, but LARRY*
> *pulls it away from him and hauls him away. All*
> *this violence happens in slow motion while "Ave*
> *Maria" plays.*

SCENE 6

Disclosure

Larry and Desdemona's house.
DESDEMONA enters with a glass of wine
and an eyepatch. She sits and begins doing eye
exercises, rolling her eyes about in big circles.
LITTLE RED WARRIOR crosses with
bandaged hands holding a roll of toilet paper;
DESDEMONA tries to get his attention.

DESDEMONA
Um, Mr. Red Warrior, sir? Um, excuse me?

DESDEMONA removes the eyepatch for
LITTLE RED WARRIOR. He scrutinizes
both her eyes and then delivers his judgment.

LITTLE RED WARRIOR
Lazy.

LITTLE RED WARRIOR exits.

DESDEMONA
Why?!

DESDEMONA sits down and drinks her
wine. LARRY enters.

LARRY
Hun? Why don't we invite Little Red up for a special
dinner tonight? He's down in the basement all by himself,
and he only comes up to go to the bathroom. I'm worried
about him. That slap on the wrist he got from the judge
seems to have really upset him. I think he's depressed, and
you know how dangerous that can be for the Natives.

> *LITTLE RED WARRIOR enters, toilet*
> *paper in hand.*

LARRY
Speak of the devil. Um, say, Red, Mona and I have been
talking … uh, why don't you join us for dinner tonight?
Mona and I would be honoured if you would.

DESDEMONA
Honoured?

> *LARRY nudges her.*

DESDEMONA
Why yes, we would be just bursting forth with honour.

LITTLE RED WARRIOR
(*looking at DESDEMONA*) Honoured, huh? What're
you cooking?

LARRY
I don't know. What do you feel like?

LITTLE RED WARRIOR
Hey, I'm the guest.

DESDEMONA
How about Indian?

LITTLE RED WARRIOR
Huh?

LARRY
You know, curried dishes and that sort of thing.

LITTLE RED WARRIOR
Oh, those Indians. I thought for a second there you
wanted me to make some bannock or something.

LARRY
We'll order out. I can go make the pickup. What about
drinks after?

DESDEMONA
Oh, I drank all the wine.

LARRY
I'll pick something up. I shouldn't be too long.

> *DESDEMONA reveals a bottle of wine from
> somewhere unexpected.*

LARRY
I thought you said you drank all the wine.

DESDEMONA
As soon as I finish this bottle, dear, all the wine
will be gone.

LARRY
You two just chit-chat a while. I'll be back shortly.

LARRY exits. Silence. DESDEMONA looks
out a window, downs the rest of her glass of
wine, and refills it. LITTLE RED WARRIOR
stares off into space, remembers he needs to use
the bathroom, and heads towards it.

DESDEMONA
What did you say?

LITTLE RED WARRIOR
What?

DESDEMONA
Nothing, I thought you said something.

LITTLE RED WARRIOR
Nope.

DESDEMONA
Oh.

> *LITTLE RED WARRIOR tries to*
> *leave again.*

DESDEMONA
So? Red. Can I call you Red? Or Chief? Or is it Chief
Little Red? Tiny Chief Warrior? Oh, to hell with this!

> *DESDEMONA downs the glass of wine and*
> *immediately refills it.*

LITTLE RED WARRIOR
Hey, what's wrong?

> *DESDEMONA starts pacing.*

DESDEMONA

Do you realize I haven't left the house since you made
your great discovery about my misaligned eyeballs?!
I haven't gone to work. I almost got fired from my job!

LITTLE RED WARRIOR

Why?

DESDEMONA

Because I've been playing hooky! How can I look
another client in the eyes? I've never lost a case in my
life. NEVER! How can I instill terror in people when my
eyeballs are all askew!

LITTLE RED WARRIOR

I didn't do anything.

DESDEMONA

And what the hell kind of name is Little Red?! Sounds like
a sex toy with an inferiority complex.

LITTLE RED WARRIOR

Hey!

DESDEMONA

You come waltzing into my home and look me in the eyes
and tell me I'm defective. You called me lazy. An Indian
called me lazy!

LITTLE RED WARRIOR

Now wait a minute! I don't need to take abuse from you.

DESDEMONA

You're looking for something, you've been plotting
something.

LITTLE RED WARRIOR
I don't know what you are talking about. I was invited to
stay here.

DESDEMONA
I never invited you! I never wanted you here. But now
you are. And I see you. Watching me. Looking at me the
way you do.

LITTLE RED WARRIOR
Are you drunk?

DESDEMONA
But don't you try anything with me, mister. I am devoted.
Do you hear me?

LITTLE RED WARRIOR
(*indicating the toilet paper*) I just wanted to use the –

DESDEMONA
I know what you want to use!

LITTLE RED WARRIOR
Whoa! Easy there. Come on. Take it easy, Mona. Lemme
get you some water.

> *DESDEMONA grabs hold of LITTLE
> RED WARRIOR and stares at him like he's
> a sandwich.*

LITTLE RED WARRIOR
Oh no ... you've had too much of the sauce. I know what
you're thinking. It's written all over your face.

DESDEMONA
What's that, Little Red? What do you see written all over my face?

LITTLE RED WARRIOR
Lust.

DESDEMONA
I'll show you lust!

LITTLE RED WARRIOR
Maybe it was the q̓ʷúne?! Fermented salmon eggs is a powerful aphrodisiac, you know!

DESDEMONA
You wanna know a little secret, Little Red?

LITTLE RED WARRIOR
I'm not sure I do. Some secrets are best kept buried. Deep down in a sandy hole –

DESDEMONA
I haven't been laid in months.

LITTLE RED WARRIOR
You *are* drunk.

DESDEMONA
Months!

LITTLE RED WARRIOR
Whatever. Check your privilege. Try years.

DESDEMONA
Years?

LITTLE RED WARRIOR
It's not like there are lots of opportunities up there in
the Red Warrior Valley, I mean, sure, there's the odd
hikers. Like maybe a young couple who gets lost, snowed
in, clothes all wet, have to take them off by the fire, all
shivering, afraid, but grateful, with goosebumps, needing
to be comforted. Next thing you know the husband is
asking you if you'd like to have a go at his wife. And then
boom! Just like that. Threesome. When it rains, it pours.

DESDEMONA
How many years?

LITTLE RED WARRIOR
Well, let's see ... there was Wendy and Don, that was
about five years ago ... Beergit. She was German ... those
Germans are nuts about Natives, let me tell you! That was
maybe four years ago –

DESDEMONA
That's pretty hard up, Little Red.

LITTLE RED WARRIOR
Whatever, I got cable.

DESDEMONA
Yeah, I bet you've got cable!

LITTLE RED WARRIOR
Uh, can I go to the bathroom now?

LITTLE RED WARRIOR tries to leave.

DESDEMONA
– Oh no, you don't get off that easily.

DESDEMONA gets in his way.

DESDEMONA
Look at me! Come on, damn it! Look me in the eye. What
do you see?

LITTLE RED WARRIOR
Didn't we already do that? I really need to use the can.

DESDEMONA
Not until you answer my question!

LITTLE RED WARRIOR
Okay! All right. I see –

DESDEMONA
What?

LITTLE RED WARRIOR
I see –

DESDEMONA
Tell me!

LITTLE RED WARRIOR
I see a woman whose heart and spirit are empty! Who
lives in a great big empty house! Working at an empty job
to fulfill her empty life! Who won't let me use her shitter
because she's so self-absorbed she's going cross-eyed!

> *DESDEMONA slaps LITTLE RED
> WARRIOR. She kisses him. LITTLE
> RED WARRIOR pulls away and exits.
> DESDEMONA is left alone. Blackout.*

SCENE 7

Steaming Hot Samosas

LITTLE RED WARRIOR, LARRY, and DESDEMONA sit at the dinner table eating Indian food.

LARRY
So, anyway, this guy walks up to the counter and says, "Can I have a cheeseburger?" Oh man. I just about lost it. Can you imagine?

DESDEMONA
(*eyeing LITTLE RED WARRIOR*) No dear, that's just bizarre.

LARRY
I mean, come on. A cheeseburger at an Indian restaurant! Some people are just not on the same planet as the rest of us. How much of a hick do you gotta be? No offence, Red.

LITTLE RED WARRIOR
None taken.

LARRY
So, hey, I think we have a pretty strong case.

LITTLE RED WARRIOR
Good.

LARRY
I have confidence. It's complicated, Red. Very complicated,
but that's why you need me, if it was easy, well, you could
just waltz into that courtroom and get the deal yourself.
You know, Mona's a pretty good lawyer, too. Maybe you
could help me on this one.

DESDEMONA
I'm busy.

LARRY
With what?

DESDEMONA
A deal of my own, thank you very much.

LARRY
Honey, this case, this settlement. It's a little more complex
than bargain condos for hipsters.

DESDEMONA
Of course, dear, what was I thinking?

LARRY
It's like this samosa here. (*taking LITTLE RED
WARRIOR's samosa off his plate*) The white man,
or settlers, if you like, came to this country and found it
like a giant juicy samosa waiting to be devoured.

LITTLE RED WARRIOR
Columbus was looking for samosas?

LARRY
Bite by bite we inched across the continent, munching
and munching away until there was nothing left to munch.
But it wasn't our samosa; it was his. See? We should give it
back. Now is the time for justice. Now is the time for his
people to stand up and hire a lawyer!

Angels begin to sing in the choir of heaven.

LARRY
We can be the redeemers of our forefathers.

LITTLE RED WARRIOR
Now you're talking.

LARRY
We can be their salvation.

LITTLE RED WARRIOR
If you say so.

LARRY
We are their guides to the Promised Land!

LITTLE RED WARRIOR
Easy now.

LARRY
We must dig down deep inside ourselves and find the
light that guides us through to righteous victory over our
oppressors.

LITTLE RED WARRIOR
Ho siem, bro!

LARRY
For this is the age of vindication.

LITTLE RED WARRIOR
Yes, it is.

LARRY
This is the age of redemption!

LITTLE RED WARRIOR
All my relations!

LARRY
This is the age of the Little Red Warrior and His Lawyer!!

The angels in the choir of heaven climax.

LARRY
Uh-oh.

LARRY collapses unconscious into his curry.

LITTLE RED WARRIOR
What the –

DESDEMONA
Roofies don't mix well with alcohol.

LITTLE RED WARRIOR
Jeezus!

DESDEMONA
I needed to talk to you, and I couldn't wait.

LITTLE RED WARRIOR
So you roofied your husband? That's not appropriate.

DESDEMONA
I can't stop thinking about you. I want to hate you, but I can't. You're using tantric Shaman sex magic, aren't you?

LITTLE RED WARRIOR
I find this scenario highly unlikely.

DESDEMONA
You put a spell on me.

> *DESDEMONA comes on to LITTLE*
> *RED WARRIOR.*

LITTLE RED WARRIOR
I'm no panty Shaman! What about your husband? You're just gonna jump me right here while your husband is passed out in his curry?

DESDEMONA
He doesn't see me, not like you do. You can see right into me, can't you?

LITTLE RED WARRIOR
What if he wakes up?

DESDEMONA
He'll be out for hours.

> *DESDEMONA tackles LITTLE*
> *RED WARRIOR.*

LITTLE RED WARRIOR
Couldn't you wait until he left the house?

DESDEMONA
It's more exciting this way.

LITTLE RED WARRIOR
Come on, this is ridiculous. I mean, who does this?!

DESDEMONA
You want to. I see the way you look at me. I can feel you
looking at me. Looking right into me. Right inside me.
Do you have any idea how sexy you are right now? Wide-
eyed and terrified.

LITTLE RED WARRIOR
We shouldn't, I can't, I want to, but that would be bad,
that's not how you treat a friend, by schtuping his wife.

DESDEMONA
He'll never know.

> DESDEMONA takes off LITTLE RED
> WARRIOR's belt.

LITTLE RED WARRIOR
Okay, okay, supposing we do this, uh, what then,
I mean, you know, we still gotta see each other every
day. Awkward ...

DESDEMONA
I like it when you're flustered.

> DESDEMONA snaps the belt like a
> dominatrix.

LITTLE RED WARRIOR
Holy shit!

DESDEMONA
We've got a lot of learning ahead of us. A lot of sharing.
Don't worry, though, I'm a good teacher.

DESDEMONA *cracks his belt again.*

LITTLE RED WARRIOR
What is with you people and belts?! Oh god, oh god ...
be gentle.

DESDEMONA *jumps onto LITTLE RED
WARRIOR, who carries her away to his room
downstairs. Red special on LARRY.*

Larry's Vision

LARRY stands with the red special from the previous scene still on him. Chanting and whispering can be heard.

LARRY
Who are you? Where am I?

FLOYD
I don't know. You tell me.

LARRY
This is a dream, right? I'm dreaming? It feels like a dream.

FLOYD
Can you feel darkness wrapping itself around you like a blanket? You must make yourself strong against the forces that would blind you.

LARRY
Uh, you lost me there.

FLOYD
Sorry, sometimes I get a bit moody and cryptic. I'm preparing you for war. Kind of a drug-induced psycho-spiritual pep talk.

LARRY
For war, oh, you mean for the court battle! Wow, is this like a vision or something?

FLOYD
The bones of the nation were forged with these words. Look to the past for the future to be found. Buried deep in the lore of the Land, a Chief made a pact with a cougar. The cougar left with the Chief in her mouth, but the Chief ran away with the spoon ...

FLOYD fades back into the darkness. As the chanting fades out, LARRY is left alone.

LARRY
The Chief ran away with the spoon? What the hell does that mean? Hello? Is my vision over now? What does it mean? Spooky!

LARRY turns and looks offstage.

LARRY
Huh, well, I guess I'll have to find my own way out of here. Thanks for ditching out! Spirit guide, my ass!

LARRY walks out of the light and stubs his toe.

LARRY
Oww! My pinky toe!

Uncle Dinky

*Lights up on LITTLE RED WARRIOR and
DESDEMONA in bed, post coitus. LITTLE
RED WARRIOR is wearing the eyepatch.*

DESDEMONA
That was ... nice.

LITTLE RED WARRIOR
Nice?

DESDEMONA
Good, nice.

LITTLE RED WARRIOR
Yeah? Well, as long as it was good-nice.

DESDEMONA
It was. Chief.

     DESDEMONA giggles.

LITTLE RED WARRIOR
What?

DESDEMONA
It just seems funny. I never thought I would ever make it
with an actual Indian Chief.

DESDEMONA giggles.

LITTLE RED WARRIOR
It's a big responsibility. I am the Chief and sole member of
the Little Red Warrior First Nation. I am the custodian of
that Land.

DESDEMONA
I'm curious about this thing you and Larry are scheming.
You haven't told me a thing about it.

LITTLE RED WARRIOR
Well, it's kind of complicated.

DESDEMONA
Well, I am a lawyer too you know. I think I can handle it.

LITTLE RED WARRIOR
Well, I'm getting booted off my Land. But we're gonna
make millions. Because my family lived there since time
in-mem-memoriable ... we're gonna take back what's mine.
And get rich or die tryin'.

DESDEMONA
Wow, I've never really had a home like that. I was always
being moved around between my parents. I grew up all
over the world. I never really felt connected to anywhere.

LITTLE RED WARRIOR
You got no roots. Maybe that's how you got lost.
Sometimes that happens, you know. People get lost.

DESDEMONA
Yeah?

LITTLE RED WARRIOR
Sometimes they get so lost even though they are
surrounded by people. Sometimes they get lost and never
come back. I lost my Uncle Dinky.

DESDEMONA
You did?

LITTLE RED WARRIOR
Yeah. One night he got drunk and wandered out into the
bush. And he never came back. Cold winter that year.
I think he just had enough.

DESDEMONA
Your uncle froze to death?

LITTLE RED WARRIOR
No, no, Uncle Dinky was a bit on the hefty side, three
hundred, three-fifty maybe, he was well insulated,
he would have been able to make it, two, maybe three
nights out there, if it hadn't been for … old Nelly.

DESDEMONA
Old Nelly?

LITTLE RED WARRIOR
Yeah, she was a cougar.

DESDEMONA
Like a cat?

LITTLE RED WARRIOR
No, a cougar! A big, old, toothy, badass, man-eating cougar! She was legendary. She preferred younger meat, but Uncle Dinky had a special charm.

DESDEMONA
Kinda like you.

LITTLE RED WARRIOR
Right?! Anyways. She'd been stalking me for about three weeks before she got Dinky.

DESDEMONA
No!

LITTLE RED WARRIOR
Oh yeah. Old Nelly stalked Uncle Dinky as he walked into the trees. He and my old man had been on a bender for about a week, when suddenly Uncle Dinky felt the spirits calling him out into the cold night. So he put on his big Kodiaks and out he went. We never saw Uncle Dinky again. Old Nelly, she took him.

DESDEMONA
Oh, Red. How horrible.

LITTLE RED WARRIOR
That is why I fight for that Land. With Dinky gone, it is my responsibility to uphold the trust. The spirits of the Red Warriors have permeated that Land for generations.

DESDEMONA
Permeated.

LITTLE RED WARRIOR
Permeated.

DESDEMONA
I want to see the world as you see it, to feel the spirits, to know your home. Teach me.

LITTLE RED WARRIOR
No. You are not ready.

DESDEMONA
Please.

LITTLE RED WARRIOR
Well, okay. I need to ask my Bovine Spirit Helper first.

DESDEMONA
Bovine? You mean like Buffalo?

LITTLE RED WARRIOR
No, I mean Bovine. The spirit of all the cow-like beasts of the world.

DESDEMONA
Ohhh …

LITTLE RED WARRIOR
Hmm.

> *LITTLE RED WARRIOR raises his hand in an attempt to look like he's searching for something deep and profound within himself.*

LITTLE RED WARRIOR
My Bovine Spirit Helper is pissed right off right now! But
he tells me that you are to be called ... Flannel Dancer.

DESDEMONA
Wow. Flannel Dancer. Is that my Aboriginal Title?

LITTLE RED WARRIOR
No. It's your Indian Name.

DESDEMONA
Flannel Dancer. What does that mean?

LITTLE RED WARRIOR
That's for you to discover.

> *LITTLE RED WARRIOR gets back into
> bed and kisses DESDEMONA. The lights
> fade to black; cue sexy music. Lights down on
> the lovers.*

SCENE 10

Epiphany

*LARRY enters. He sits at the table and begins
writing on papers and reading books and/or
online documents.*

LARRY

Terra nullius, the doctrine of discovery ... Natives
were considered non-human because they weren't
Christian? Hmm. Therefore, any Lands they occupied
were considered empty of human habitation ... and
were therefore free for the taking ... *Terra nullius!* Then
the Royal Proclamation of 1763. "No territories shall be
claimed by the crown without the consent of the resident
native Indians acquired through the due process of treaty
negotiation ..." The British North American Act, 1867,
which leads to the Constitution Act, which leads to ... the
Indian Act! Numbered Treaties, Potlatch ban, residential
schools. Natives get the vote in 1960 ... finally considered
persons under the law ... 1960?! Then, Meech Lake
Accord ... Elijah Harper's Great Big No! Delgamuukw!
Sparrow v. the Queen! Tsilhqot'in v. British Columbia!
Holy shit! "Look into the past for the future to be found!"
It's all here! It's all happening right in front of our eyes.
Huh, where have I been all this time?

Lights fade on LARRY.

SCENE 11

Reflection

FLOYD enters.

FLOYD
While Larry poured over ancient legal documents and precedent-setting court cases ...

> *DESDEMONA enters in a "Lone Ranger" cowboy hat and mask, with cap gun ablazing, chasing LITTLE RED WARRIOR in sexy/ offensive "Pocahontas" lingerie.*

FLOYD
Little Red was getting laid. Desdemona was discovering something new, spontaneous, and exciting ... while Larry was being cuckolded. On the surface, everything seemed –

LARRY
(*looking up from his papers*) Perfect! I'm good. I'm so bloody good.

> *Lights up on LITTLE RED WARRIOR watching TV, sitting in an armchair.*

LITTLE RED WARRIOR
I'm so bad.

LARRY begins organizing his mess of papers.

LARRY
For once in my life, I have purpose!

LITTLE RED WARRIOR
I'm screwing his wife, in his own house, wearing his cowboy boots. I'm surprised they fit.

LARRY
I'm the righteous prosecutor of wrongdoers to all the Red Warriors of the world.

LITTLE RED WARRIOR
This can't be good for my Karma Sutra. (*changing channel*) Hey, Home Shopping Network.

LARRY
I will prey on the guilt of a nation.

LITTLE RED WARRIOR
It's so bad –

LARRY
I will draw on the tears of a people.

LITTLE RED WARRIOR
But it feels so good.

LARRY
I will resurrect the ghosts of all those who dreamed of a better world. I will conjure up the spirits of Geronimo and Gandhi and make them dance in that courtroom.

LITTLE RED WARRIOR
It's like I'm John Smith. And she's Pocahontas. But
in reverse.

Lights up on DESDEMONA, stage right,
looking into a mirror.

DESDEMONA
I wonder if he suspects. I wonder if he can tell.

LITTLE RED WARRIOR
Whatever! I'm getting what's owed me.

DESDEMONA
I feel different.

LITTLE RED WARRIOR
I deserve this.

LARRY
(*singing*) "O, Canada! Our home on Native Land!"

LITTLE RED WARRIOR
(*flipping channels*) Things. Lots of things.

DESDEMONA
(*looking into a mirror*) I look different.

LITTLE RED WARRIOR
Big. Shiny. Expensive things.

LARRY
It's not about the money.

LITTLE RED WARRIOR
It's all about the money.

LARRY
It's time. Time for a change. For the better. For
something ... real!

> *LITTLE RED WARRIOR furiously changes
> the channels.*

LITTLE RED WARRIOR
She can smell it. She can smell that money coming my
way. That's why she wants me.

> *DESDEMONA stops and stares at herself in
> the mirror.*

DESDEMONA
What am I doing?

LITTLE RED WARRIOR
My people have suffered. I have suffered.

DESDEMONA
Who am I?

LARRY
I am that change.

DESDEMONA
I'm so sick of this face.

> *DESDEMONA begins painting her face like
> a warrior.*

LITTLE RED WARRIOR
I deserve this.

LARRY
A brave new world –

DESDEMONA
No more emptiness.

LITTLE RED WARRIOR
I gotta play my cards right.

LARRY
Anything is possible.

Lights down on LARRY.

LITTLE RED WARRIOR
I deserve it. All of it.

*Lights down on LITTLE RED WARRIOR.
DESDEMONA is left alone staring at herself
in the mirror. A pretendian warrior.*

DESDEMONA
There I am. No more lies. Free.

*DESDEMONA takes off her wedding ring.
LARRY enters her space.*

LARRY
Honey? What're you doing?

*DESDEMONA quickly wipes off her
war paint.*

DESDEMONA
I was just –

LARRY
Who were you talking to?

DESDEMONA
Nobody … no one. I was just talking to myself.

LARRY
I'm going to bed, you coming?

DESDEMONA
No. I need to finish up some work I brought home.
Remember that case I was –

LARRY
Oh, yeah, right, uh, bargain condos for hipsters or some
silly – um, tell me about it after tomorrow, okay dear?
I've got a lot on my mind right now. Hurry up and
come to bed.

>   *LARRY goes to exit.*

DESDEMONA
Larry, about tomorrow, I want to –

LARRY
Don't worry, honey, we'll have everything we always
wanted. I will buy you the biggest and the best of
everything … things, lots and lots of things …

>   *LARRY exits. DESDEMONA finishes wiping
>   off the war paint as the lights go down.*

SCENE 12

Courtship

FLOYD stands centre stage putting on his judicial robes.

FLOYD
Well, finally the day had come. Larry and Red's case was ready for trial. Larry was ready to give the best fight of his legal career.

FLOYD puts on a white wig and becomes LOWER COURT FLOYD. LARRY and LITTLE RED WARRIOR enter. Larry looks as though he's preparing to enter a boxing ring. He's wearing a suit and tie and LITTLE RED WARRIOR is massaging his shoulders, warming him up. DESDEMONA enters. She walks over to LITTLE RED WARRIOR and LARRY.

LARRY
Hi, honey. What are you doing here?

DESDEMONA
Good luck.

> DESDEMONA *shakes* LARRY's *hand, gives*
> LITTLE RED WARRIOR *a look, and then*
> *walks back to stage right.*

LOWER COURT FLOYD
I see that the representative for Smith, Smyth, and
Goldesmithe has arrived. We shall proceed?

LITTLE RED WARRIOR
She's the enemy?!

LARRY
Honey, what is this? What are you doing?

DESDEMONA
Smith, Smyth, and Goldesmithe have retained the services
of my firm. If I win this case, they'll make me senior
partner. I'm sorry Red, nothing personal, it's just business.

LITTLE RED WARRIOR
Yeah. Business.

LARRY
But this is a conflict of interest! Conflict of interest!

LOWER COURT FLOYD
And just whose interests are conflicted?

LARRY
Hers! She can't go to trial against me; we're married!

DESDEMONA
Your Honour, I want a divorce.

LOWER COURT FLOYD
Oh, and why is that, sweetheart?

DESDEMONA
Because, Your Honourableness, my husband is
incompetent and ...

LOWER COURT FLOYD
Yes?

DESDEMONA
Impotent.

LOWER COURT FLOYD
Oh well, well. There's a pill for that! And who is your
husband, little missy?

DESDEMONA
(*pointing to LARRY*) He is, Your Honour.

LOWER COURT FLOYD
Mmm hmm, right, I see. Well, okay, if you say so. By the
powers bestowed upon me by the almighty hammer of
justice, I now pronounce you ex-man and ex-wife.

LOWER COURT FLOYD bangs his gavel.

LARRY
Honey! No!

LOWER COURT FLOYD
Get a grip! Order! Order! Another outburst like that,
young man, and I'll have you hung!

DESDEMONA
It's just business, Larry. I've never lost a case.

LARRY
I've been working on this case for months! You haven't got a chance!

DESDEMONA
So have I, Larry. So have I.

LOWER COURT FLOYD
Shall we begin? All right then, as I'm sure you know, this case would normally take ages to litigate, racking up enormous financial benefits for you and your firm whilst grinding your Indigenous opponent into mortal poverty. Luckily, I've devised a new type of procedure with which to deal with this, quote, Lands Claim issue. I'll give you each about a minute to make your case, after which I'll think about it. If I'm not convinced either way, well then, I don't know what we'll do. And if I don't know what to do, then we won't do anything.

LARRY
Sounds good to me.

LITTLE RED WARRIOR
What?!

LOWER COURT FLOYD
Silence! I am the all-powerful one here. And if you won't obey my authority, then the great hammer will fall upon you!

DESDEMONA
I am ready to present my case, Your Honourably
Honourable, for my clients, the developers, Smith,
Smyth, and Goldesmithe.

LOWER COURT FLOYD
Ooh my, yes, well all right, sweetheart. Carry forth thy
duties. You may approach the bench ...

DESDEMONA as FLANNEL DANCER
Flannel Dancer.

LOWER COURT FLOYD
Please proceed at your leisure, Flannel Dancer.

LARRY
Flannel Dancer?

LITTLE RED WARRIOR
It's like a sexy snuggle.

LOWER COURT FLOYD
PROCEED!

FLANNEL DANCER
First, I would like to acknowledge that we are on stolen
Land. But that our Ancestors wanted us to steal it. And
so we did. I just want to acknowledge that. So thank you.
For the Land.

LOWER COURT FLOYD
Beautiful. Meaningful. Proceed.

FLANNEL DANCER
Your Honour. Blah blah blah, Doctrine of Discovery.
Blah ha ha, Comprehensive Land Claims. Blah ha ha ha.
Blubla blah. Therefore, blaha blaha, Termination Plan,
blaha ha ha.

LOWER COURT FLOYD
Ha ha ha ha ha!

FLANNEL DANCER
Ha ha! Ha ha.

LOWER COURT FLOYD
You make a very well-rounded argument, my dear! A very
strong argument indeed! In fact, your arguments have
reached down into the core of who I am, and I find it very
hard to be swayed in any direction other than that of the
argument you have so eloquently orated just now to my
face. Thank you. Truly. Thank you.

LARRY
Your Honourest, I object.

LOWER COURT FLOYD
Overruled.

LARRY
Your Honourestness is displaying biases.

> *LOWER COURT FLOYD stares
> down at LARRY.*

LOWER COURT FLOYD
Am not.

LARRY
Am.

LOWER COURT FLOYD
Am. Not.

LARRY
Am ... not.

LOWER COURT FLOYD
Yes, good ... good. Now the representative for the Little
Red Warrior. Proceed.

LARRY
I, too, would like to thank –

LOWER COURT FLOYD
Nope! We're not hearing that. We acknowledged already,
let's get on with it!

LITTLE RED WARRIOR
Hey! This is disrespectful!

LOWER COURT FLOYD
Is it?!

LITTLE RED WARRIOR
Yeah!

> *LOWER COURT FLOYD stairs down at
> LITTLE RED WARRIOR. LITTLE RED
> WARRIOR is resolute.*

LOWER COURT FLOYD
You're right. I'm sorry. I'm so sorry. I'm so, so sorry. Will
you ever forgive me?

LITTLE RED WARRIOR
I ... guess so ...

LOWER COURT FLOYD
Yes. Good ... good. Now, the representative for the Little
Red Warrior ...

LARRY
Larry. Your Honour.

LOWER COURT FLOYD
Larry.

LARRY
The Lawyer.

LOWER COURT FLOYD
Larry the Lawyer. Please. Proceed.

LARRY
Uh, right, Your Honour. Blah blah blah –

LOWER COURT FLOYD
Thank you, thank you very much, I think I've
heard enough.

LARRY
But Your Honour!

LOWER COURT FLOYD
Don't you talk back to me, boy! What do you think this is,
some third-rate banana republic where you can just make
up the rules as you go along?! No! I make up the rules!

LARRY
But –

LOWER COURT FLOYD
Zip it! Zip! It! And now I will deliberate. Very carefully.
On this very important matter, thus to make my
precedent-setting decision.

> *Beat.*

Well, I've thought it over, and I've decided somebody
should really remedy this situation. Here is a list of things
that I think should happen.

> *LOWER COURT FLOYD pulls out a big-ass
> scroll, which unfurls onto the floor.*

LOWER COURT FLOYD
Somebody should go through this list and do all those
things I mention therein; who that somebody is I don't
know. But somebody better do something before this
issue gets out of hand, etc., etc. Oh sorry, this is the wrong
document, this is the one I wrote for the last time this
nonsense came up, ah, here we are.

> *LOWER COURT FLOYD unfurls an
> identical scroll.*

This here is an exact replica of the decision made several decades ago regarding this very same issue, but you'll note it has today's date on it, and this one does not, thereby making my findings current. So there. Happy?

LITTLE RED WARRIOR
But what have you decided? Who has title to the Land?

LOWER COURT FLOYD
Hell, I don't know! On the one hand, you clearly have a historic and legally binding claim to this particular piece of property, but on the other hand ... too bad. We're here now, and you just need to get over it. This court is not equipped and/or not willing to endure the unravelling of this colonial construct. So ... tough titty said the kitty when the milk went dry.

LITTLE RED WARRIOR
What?!

LARRY
Red, calm down, we can still appeal –

LOWER COURT FLOYD
Oh, yes of course, appeal, if you must.

LARRY
Your Honourhood, we formally request an appeal.

LOWER COURT FLOYD
Sure. No problem.

> LOWER COURT FLOYD takes off his wig
> and puts on an even bigger wig, becoming
> APPEALS COURT FLOYD.

APPEALS COURT FLOYD
What are your arguments?

DESDEMONA
The same, Your Honour.

APPEALS COURT FLOYD
And you?

LARRY
I –

APPEALS COURT FLOYD
This Court of Appeal hereby upholds the previous
decision to do nothing on this matter, thereby allowing
the developers to do whatever the fuck they want. Case
adjourned.

LARRY
Your Honour, we challenge –

APPEALS COURT FLOYD
Supreme Court? Not to worry.

> *APPEALS COURT FLOYD dons an even
> larger wig that nearly obscures his head,
> becoming SUPREME COURT FLOYD.*

SUPREME COURT FLOYD
I, the supreme officer of justice residing in the most
powerful court of law on these our Lands, uphold that the
decisions made by the lower, smaller, more insignificant
courts must be upheld. So sayeth I in my super-deluxe
supremeness. Forever and eva-eva – until tomorrow and
then some more.

LARRY
But Your Honour, that solves nothing!

SUPREME COURT FLOYD
Of course it solves nothing! This court is not here to solve
your problems. It is here to serve the crown. To stall the
eventual outcomes of these inconveniences to the benefit,
interests, and goals of the crown. In all its glory.

> *An awesome giant crown is projected or hangs
> above the audience throughout this scene. How
> it gets there is anyone's guess.*

LARRY
Justice?

SUPREME COURT FLOYD
Justice? Don't be naive! The crown! The crown! All hail
the mighty crown!

> *SUPREME COURT FLOYD, DESDEMONA,
> and LARRY all bow to the crown. LITTLE
> RED WARRIOR does not.*

LITTLE RED WARRIOR
I knew it! The crown! You know who belongs to that
crown? The Queen!

> *LITTLE RED WARRIOR begins to draw
> a large crown on the floor of the courthouse
> with white chalk. The stage is awash in
> fire; the moans of the unavenged Ancestors
> can be heard.*

SUPREME COURT FLOYD
What in hell are you doing?! And what is that noise?!

LITTLE RED WARRIOR
That's the moans of the unavenged Ancestors of the
Little Red Warriors! The mothers and fathers, sisters and
brothers, uncles and aunties, and grandmas and grandpas!
Who fought and lost and were forgotten. Forgotten by all
of you! Now keep your honourable trap shut or I'll pop
you one. Got it? Now we do it Oka style! Lasagna!

LARRY
Red, what are you doing?

LITTLE RED WARRIOR
I summon the Queen!

> LITTLE RED WARRIOR reaches into his
> medicine pouch and throws some magic powder
> into the centre of the completed penta-crown.
> There is a flash of fire, a plume of smoke, and
> then blackout. Slowly the lights flicker back on,
> revealing THE QUEEN, who emerges from the
> smoke in the centre of the penta-crown.

SCENE 13

Royalty

THE QUEEN
All hail the Queen, bitches!

A heavy house or drum-and-bass version of
"God Save the Queen" plays. Laser lights and
strobes flash like in a dance club on a Saturday
night as THE QUEEN sashays back and
forth across the stage within the confines of the
penta-crown.

THE QUEEN
Long live the Queen! She's a dance machine! Is that
my heel on your neck? Let me write you a cheque. For
all your pain and neglect, dahling! Now give it back to
me! Slut! It was mine, anyways. See, my picture's on the
money. That's how you know who's your mummy. It is I,
the Queen!

THE QUEEN sees LITTLE RED
WARRIOR and reacts like a blood-
lusting vampire.

THE QUEEN
Hsssss! Indian!

THE QUEEN, hissing, with claws out, tries
to attack LITTLE RED WARRIOR, but is
contained by the penta-crown drawn on the
courtroom floor. Her outstretched arms grasp
and claw at LITTLE RED WARRIOR.

DESDEMONA
Red! Watch out!

LITTLE RED WARRIOR
Don't worry, I've got her contained. I should have done
this from the beginning.

LARRY
What the hell is going on?

THE QUEEN hisses and vogues at LITTLE
RED WARRIOR. Fire belches from the depths
beneath her.

LITTLE RED WARRIOR
Lizzy. It's me. Little Red. Little Red Warrior of the Red
Warrior First Indians. Remember? Do you remember the
Little Red First Indians?

THE QUEEN
Why yesssss, dahling. I remember you. Little Red Warrior.
Why have you summoned me?

LITTLE RED WARRIOR
I've got a problem I was hoping you could help me with.

THE QUEEN
Are you aware of the consequences of invoking my
assistance?

LITTLE RED WARRIOR
Yes. I am.

THE QUEEN
Oh, well, well then ... Winner, winner, chicken dinner.
Whisper your desires in my ear. My pretty. Little.
Red. Warrior.

    DESDEMONA and LARRY huddle away
    from the madness.

DESDEMONA
This is nuts.

LARRY
You divorced me over this? How could you sell out our
marriage for a corporation? I have no idea who you are.

DESDEMONA
No, Larry, you don't.

LITTLE RED WARRIOR
Hey, you! (*gesturing to SUPREME COURT FLOYD*) The
Queen wants to talk to you.

SUPREME COURT FLOYD
This is madness! I will not be accosted in my own court!
Do you hear me? Do you –

    THE QUEEN throws up her hand and
    suddenly SUPREME COURT FLOYD can't
    speak, in fact, he can't even breathe. He clutches
    at his throat. THE QUEEN vogues in his
    direction.

THE QUEEN
Listen, bitch. You see that delicious Little Red Warrior
over there? He's got me by the balls. You see. We're in
a relationship. That predates this little arrangement. So,
if you could give back what belongs to him. I'd appreciate
it. Capisce?

SUPREME COURT FLOYD
You mean give him his Land back?!

THE QUEEN
Are you questioning me?!

SUPREME COURT FLOYD
No, Your Majesty! Grand Deity of the Colonies!

THE QUEEN
On your knees.

SUPREME COURT FLOYD
Yes, Your Majesty!

THE QUEEN
Kiss my shoes.

SUPREME COURT FLOYD
Yes, Your Majesty!

*SUPREME COURT FLOYD kisses THE
QUEEN's shoes.*

THE QUEEN
For as long as the wind blows, the grass grows,
and the water flows, these Lands are your Lands
forevermore. Say it.

SUPREME COURT FLOYD
For as long as the wind blows, the grass grows, and the
water flows, these Lands are your Lands forevermore.

THE QUEEN
Say it to him.

SUPREME COURT FLOYD
I –

THE QUEEN
SAY IT!

SUPREME COURT FLOYD
(*to LITTLE RED WARRIOR*) For as long as the wind
blows, the grass grows, and the water flows, these Lands
are your Lands forevermore.

THE QUEEN
Say it like you mean it.

SUPREME COURT FLOYD
For as long as the wind blows, the grass grows, and the
water flows, these Lands are your Lands forevermore!

THE QUEEN
Good boy. That wasn't so bad now, was it? Kisses.

> *SUPREME COURT FLOYD kisses THE*
> *QUEEN's feet.*

THE QUEEN
(*to LITTLE RED WARRIOR*) Now. Release me. Release
me from this pitiful setting. Send me back to my realm.
This place is cramping my fabulous.

*LITTLE RED WARRIOR takes out his chalk
and draws a corridor towards the audience.
He then breaks the seal of the penta-crown on
the floor. The house or drum-and-bass version
of "God Save the Queen" plays, lights flicker,
and THE QUEEN sashays out through the
house, vogueing with her arms as she exits.*

THE QUEEN
Remember, Red. Now you owe me. So long, bitches!

THE QUEEN exits.

SCENE 14

Trick or Treaty

LARRY
What just happened? I don't get what just happened?!

LITTLE RED WARRIOR
The Crown has spoken. Tell them.

SUPREME COURT FLOYD
In adherence to all of the laws upon which this country
was founded, the disputed Land ...

DESDEMONA
Yes?

SUPREME COURT FLOYD
Is Red Warrior Land.

LITTLE RED WARRIOR
For as long as the wind blows, the grass grows, and the
water flows. Now, if you'll excuse me, I've got some
business to take care of.

LARRY
Business?

LITTLE RED WARRIOR
I've got a meeting with a mining company.

LARRY
What?!

LITTLE RED WARRIOR
Yeah. Turns out there's a huge uranium deposit under the
lake. We're gonna drain it and strip-mine the whole valley.
Oh, not to mention that pipeline we're running through
the north end of the territory.

DESDEMONA and LARRY
What?!

LITTLE RED WARRIOR
It's in the interests of my people.

DESDEMONA
– But what about your obligations to your Ancestors,
to Uncle Dinky?

LITTLE RED WARRIOR
Uncle Dinky lives in Florida with Old Nelly –

DESDEMONA
But Old Nelly was a cougar ... ohhhh.

LITTLE RED WARRIOR
Yeah, anyways, he married out, so he had to get out.
He left home to be with her, so he can lie in that warm
tropical bed he's made. But if he thinks he's getting any of
my hard-earned Band money, he can kiss my Red –

LARRY
– But what about our deal?!

LITTLE RED WARRIOR
You didn't win the day! I did. So technically, I don't have to share. (*trying to leave*)

LARRY
What about your responsibility to the Land?

LITTLE RED WARRIOR
Hey, what about my responsibility to me?

DESDEMONA
Red, take me with you. I'll be your people.

LITTLE RED WARRIOR
Yeah ... no.

LARRY
You want to go with him?

LITTLE RED WARRIOR
You're the enemy.

DESDEMONA
(*holding LITTLE RED WARRIOR's arm*) Please –

LARRY
Will somebody please tell me what the hell is going on here?

DESDEMONA
Red –

LITTLE RED WARRIOR
You people are all alike, trying to screw me over even when you're helping me.

DESDEMONA
Red, please, listen to me –

LARRY
I busted my balls for you!

LITTLE RED WARRIOR
Yeah right, your balls couldn't bust anything, limpy-
ass cracker!

LARRY
Why, you self-serving savage –

LITTLE RED WARRIOR
Who you calling self-serving?!

LARRY
You wouldn't have anything if it weren't for me!

LITTLE RED WARRIOR
You didn't give me anything! That Land is mine! Always
was, always will be!

LARRY
I took you into my home. You screwed me over!

LITTLE RED WARRIOR
Isn't that your custom? I was just following Protocol!

LARRY
What?

LITTLE RED WARRIOR
To you, I was just a hillbilly in the bush. Poor, ignorant, helpless. You thought I needed you to survive, but I've been watching, and I've learned your ways.

DESDEMONA
Red, please, listen –

LITTLE RED WARRIOR
I see how this world works. Greed, money, power: these are your spirit helpers. I know how to call on them now. It's my turn. And I want it all.

DESDEMONA
Red, please don't do this. I … I could help you come up with a better way of managing your resources. I could help you.

LITTLE RED WARRIOR
Help me help you to understand that I AM the Land! And what the Land says goes! And right now …

LITTLE RED WARRIOR listens to the Land.

LITTLE RED WARRIOR
The Land says, *"Strip-Mine Me!!"*

DESDEMONA
No, it doesn't! This is not the way it's supposed to end!

LARRY
You wouldn't dare!

LITTLE RED WARRIOR
I double-dog dare!

LARRY
You double-dealing –

LITTLE RED WARRIOR
White devil!

> *LITTLE RED WARRIOR and LARRY*
> *break into a fist fight. DESDEMONA*
> *struggles to break it up, fails, and then ...*

DESDEMONA
Stop! I'm pregnant!

> *Silence.*

FLOYD
Of course she is.

LARRY and LITTLE RED WARRIOR
What?

LARRY
You're pregnant? We're ... Oh baby! That's ... that's
wonderful, that's a miracle. You can't leave me now
when we're going to have a ... wait, I don't ... I didn't,
I couldn't ...

> *LARRY turns to LITTLE RED WARRIOR.*

LARRY
You.

LITTLE RED WARRIOR
She's crazy!

LARRY
You?

DESDEMONA
Larry, don't …

LARRY
You.

LITTLE RED WARRIOR
Looks like you got some issues to work out, so I'll just be heading on back home.

DESDEMONA
I should have told you. I should have told you everything but … I'm an asshole.

LARRY
Or a sociopath.

LITTLE RED WARRIOR
Could be.

LARRY
I … was fighting for you … and you … she's pregnant with your … and I'm …

LITTLE RED WARRIOR
Literally a liberal cuck.

LARRY
Wow. Okay. So, like, how often were you?

LITTLE RED WARRIOR
Multiple.

LARRY
Multiple? Like, how multiple?

LITTLE RED WARRIOR
Multiple.

DESDEMONA
Multiple. Larry. Multiple.

LARRY
Oh.

> *LARRY digests the realization.*

Oh.

> *LARRY looks at the two of them. He looks
> down at his crotch.*

Wow.

DESDEMONA
Are you ...? Is that? Oh. Oh dear.

LARRY
Yeah.

LITTLE RED WARRIOR
Hola!

LARRY
Maybe ... things will work out?

LITTLE RED WARRIOR
What? You mean?

LARRY
Maybe ... we can work something out?

DESDEMONA
Really?

LARRY
Yeah.

LITTLE RED WARRIOR
Really?

LARRY
Yeah. Really.

LITTLE RED WARRIOR
Well ... all right, then. But I'm on top.

> *LITTLE RED WARRIOR, LARRY, and*
> *DESDEMONA exit together.*

SCENE 15

Epilogue

SUPREME COURT FLOYD removes his wig and becomes FLOYD.

FLOYD
Didn't see that coming, did you? Well, no matter.
It doesn't last. Time passes, seasons change, and people
change within them. Red became quite the businessman.

LITTLE RED WARRIOR appears up centre, smiling, in a suit jacket and a white hard hat.

FLOYD
He appeared on the covers of all the major magazines
and newspapers; he was filthy rich now, an example
of Indigenous economic success for all to see. And
he was right; the people could smell the money on
him. He reeked of it. Larry the Lawyer joined the
environmental movement protesting large-scale
development of any and every strip of Land with a tree
or two upon it. He tended to be most zealous about
protecting Land threatened by Indigenous developers.

LARRY enters in a flannel work shirt, handing out flyers that read, "Save the Little Red Valley."

LARRY
Save the Little Red Valley! Save the Little Red Valley!

DESDEMONA enters holding a baby.

FLOYD
Desdemona took a break from work to raise her and Little Red's baby. Raising the next generation of Little Red Warriors filled her spirit. But even as she cared for her own Little Warrior, she and Red grew distant. While Desdemona and Larry searched wholeheartedly for a more holistic lifestyle, Little Red was consumed by his new-found power and ambition.

LITTLE RED WARRIOR sees LARRY protesting and gets a shovel.

LARRY
Save the Little Red Valley! Save the Little Red Valley! Save the Little Red Valley!

LITTLE RED WARRIOR hits LARRY on the back of the head with the shovel, knocking him out cold.

FLOYD
But that is another story.

Drum and bass. THE QUEEN appears up centre, vogueing in her light. Strobes and lasers.

Blackout.

ACKNOWLEDGMENTS

Thanks to Studio 58, Western Canada Theatre, Full Circle: First Nations Performance, the First Peoples' Cultural Council, the National Arts Centre / Centre national des arts, the BC Arts Council, the Vancouver East Cultural Centre, Massey Theatre, Chelsea McPeake-Carlson, Tai Amy Grauman, Lori Marchand, John Lazarus, Stuart Pierre, Corey Turner, Sonja Bennett, David Richmond-Peck, Kathryn Shaw, Sam Bob, Dave Deveau, Craig Erickson, Luisa Jojic, Shekhar Paleja, Joshua Drebit, Pippa Mackie, Margo Kane, Jody-Kay Marklew, Jan Hodgson, Billy Merasty, and Kevin Williams.

Photo: Ian Redd

KEVIN LORING was appointed the inaugural artistic director of Indigenous Theatre at the National Arts Centre of Canada in 2017. He is Nlaka'pamux from the Lytton First Nation in British Columbia. He's a graduate of Studio 58, snəẃeyəɬ leləm̓ Langara College's Professional Theatre Training Program, and Full Circle: First Nations Performance Aboriginal Ensemble Program. He's an accomplished actor, playwright, and director, and the founding artistic director of Savage Production Society. He is the recipient of multiple awards, including the 2005 Vancouver Arts Award for Emerging Theatre Artist, the 2007 Herman Voaden Playwrighting Prize, the Sydney J. Risk Prize, the Jessie Richardson Award for Outstanding Original Script, and the 2009 Governor General's Literary Award for English-Language Drama for his first published play, *Where the Blood Mixes*. He is also the recipient of the 2010 Governor General's Performing Arts Mentorship Award. In the fall of 2017, Kevin directed the world premiere of his play *Thanks for Giving* (published by Talonbooks) at the Arts Club Theatre in Vancouver. This play was also a finalist for the 2019 Governor General's Literary Award for English-Language Drama.